Hubble the Cat

- Breed: Himalayan
- Home: Lives with the Monroes
- Dream Goal: World domination
- Admires: Anyone who feeds him
- Strength: Smart
- Weakness: Tuna and naps
- Secret: Lives for tummy rubs
- Hobby: Stowing away in knapsacks
- Techy Tool: His nose

Marina Mon

- Age 11, 6th grade
- Dream Goal: Travel to Mars
- Favorite Subject: Astronomy
- Admires: Amelia Earhart, first woman to fly solo over Atlantic Ocean
- Strength: Athletic (she has a black belt in Karate)
- Weakness: Doesn't always get jokes.
- Secret: Hates snakes
- Hobby: Stargazing
- Techy Tool: Telescope

- Dream Goal: Not sure yet!
- Favorite Subject: Earth Science
- Admires: Rachel Carson, author and environmentalist
- Strength: Leadership
- Weakness: Can't fold laundry
- Secret: Eats chocolate chips out of the bag
- Hobby: Bird-watching
- Techy Tool: Her trusty laptop

Lucy Lareau

geeky f@b 5 ®

Lucy

Zara

Marina

A.J.

Sofia

Hubble

PAPERCUTZ™

MORE GREAT GRAPHIC NOVEL
SERIES AVAILABLE FROM PAPERCUTZ

THE SMURFS TALES #1

BRINA THE CAT #1

CAT & CAT #1

THE SISTERS #1

ATTACK OF THE STUFF

ASTERIX #1

THE LOUD HOUSE #1

LOLA'S SUPER CLUB #1

THE MYTHICS #1

GUMBY #1

MELOWY #1

BLUEBEARD

DINOSAUR EXPLORERS #1

THE LITTLE MERMAID

FUZZY BASEBALL #1

ASTRO MOUSE
AND LIGHT BULB #1

GERONIMO STILTON
REPORTER #1

SCHOOL FOR EXTRA-
TERRESTRIAL GIRLS #1

X-VENTURE
XPLORERS #1

THE ONLY LIVING
GIRL #1

papercutz.com
Also available where ebooks are sold.

geeky f@b 5 ®

#5 "Smoky Mountain Science Squad"

LUCY & LIZ LAREAU — Writers
RYAN JAMPOLE — Artist

PAPERCUTZ™
NEW YORK

geeky f@b 5

#5 "Smoky Mountain Science Squad"

LUCY & LIZ LAREAU—Writers
RYAN JAMPOLE—Artist
LAURIE E. SMITH—Colorist
WILSON RAMOS JR.—Letterer
JENNIFER HERNANDEZ—Cover Artist
JEFF WHITMAN—Managing Editor
JIM SALICRUP
Editor-in-Chief

Hardcover ISBN 978-1-5458-0562-6
Paperback ISBN 978-1-5458-0561-9

Printed in Turkey Elma Basım
June 2021

Papercutz books may be purchased for business or promotional use.
For information on bulk purchases, please contact Macmillan Corporate and Premium Sales Department at (800) 221-7945 x5442.

Distributed by Macmillan
First Printing

Teacher's Guide available at:
http://papercutz.com/educator-resources-papercutz

CHAPTER ONE: LAZY SUMMER DAYS

"*LUCY MONROE* HERE. ON HOT SUMMER DAYS, MY *FAVE* LAZY SPOT IS MY HAMMOCK. *DAD* STRUNG IT IN OUR BACKYARD JUST FOR ME...

I HOPE SUMMER VACATION NEVER ENDS, *HUBBLE.* I'M SO NOT MOVING UNTIL SCHOOL STARTS.

WELL, DON'T MOVE UNTIL I'M DONE. CHERRY IS SO *PURRFECT*...

SLURP!

WHAT THE--?!

PLOP

BUZZZ

SOFIA

HI, LUCY! I'VE GOT NEWS! GET ON A CALL WITH ALL OF US... HEY, ARE YOU OKAY?

THAT'S GRAVITY FOR YOU.

YEAH. FINE... JUST GOT ATTACKED BY AN ACORN...

*CHECK OUT GEEKY FAB FIVE #3 *"DOGGONE CAT*ATROPHE" AND FIND OUT WHAT A NAUGHTY KITTY HUBBLE IS...

10

11

FAB FIVE. WE'RE THE GEEKY FAB 5! I HOPE DAD SAYS OKAY.

OH, MY GOSH. SO FUN! DO YOU THINK WE'LL BE ABLE TO GO?

BY MY COUNT, THERE AREN'T ENOUGH BEDS. THERE ARE THREE IN SOFIA'S FAMILY, PLUS FOUR OF US.

THAT EQUALS 7 PEOPLE FOR A BUNK AND TWO BEDS. WE WON'T FIT! I'M *NOT* SLEEPING ON THE GROUND!

ZARA, YOU ARE A MATH WHIZ! SO, WE CAN ALWAYS BRING A TENT. 'BELLE AND I ARE IN THE CAMPER.

NO PROB. LUCY AND I LOVE THE OUTDOORS. WE'LL SLEEP UNDER THE STARS AND TREES. IT'S CAMPING!

YEAH, AND I'LL SLEEP OUTSIDE IF ZARA WANTS THE BUNK. C'MON, ZARA...

HMMM....

I'M GOING TO MISS HOME A LOT...

OKAY! I'M IN!

CHAPTER TWO: ROADTRIPPIN'

"WITH OUR PARENT'S PERMISSION, WE KICKED INTO PACKING, PLANNING, AND YES, CLEANING MODE. WE WERE LEAVING IN A WEEK AND WE WERE SO EXCITED TO VISIT OUR FIRST NATIONAL PARK!

WHEW!, THIS OLD CAMPER IS SO DUSTY! I HOPE WE HAVE WI-FI FOR MOVIES. HEY, WHAT ARE YOU DOING?

SEWING NEW CURTAINS. YOU KNOW ME. I HAVE TO DECORATE. ABUELO WON'T CARE.

AT LEAST I *HOPE* HE LIKES PINK...

SO WE LIVE IN THE MIDDLE OF ILLINOIS... WE'LL DRIVE THROUGH INDIANA...

...KENTUCKY, AND DOWN INTO TENNESSEE AND NORTH CAROLINA. GREGORIO SAYS IT'S ABOUT 12 HOURS.

MARINA, THERE ARE A ZILLION MILES OF HIKING TRAILS. WE COULD EVEN SEE BEARS! YOU CAN HIKE TO THE TALLEST TREE IN THE WHOLE PARK. IT'S LIKE 500 YEARS OLD!

AND GUESS WHAT? WHILE WE ARE THERE A JILLION LIGHTNING BUGS COME OUT AND BLINK AT THE SAME TIME!

ROAD ATLAS

PARK GUIDE

COOL BEANS. AND I'M DEFINITELY BRINGING MY TELESCOPE. THE STAR CHARTS SAY THERE'S A COMET THAT VISITS EARTH ONCE EVERY 6,000 YEARS WE MIGHT SEE IF WE'RE LUCKY!

"MOM DROVE US OVER TO SOFIA'S HOUSE AND WE MADE IT JUST IN TIME!"

HAVE FUN! SEND US PICTURES! SAY 'PLEASE' AND 'THANK YOU.'

LOVE YOU!

LOVE YOU! BYE!

YOU GIRLS READY TO HIT THE ROAD?

YES!

MAYBE I SHOULD'VE STAYED HOME...? NAH!

"AS THE SUN CAME UP, WE HEADED EAST, TOWARD MAGICAL MISTY MOUNTAINS, GIANT TREES, AND ADVENTURE..."

WHAT THE HECK?

HUBBLE?!

YOU SNEAKY CAT!

18

SO, WHERE ARE WE NOW?

WE PASSED INDIANAPOLIS, AND WE'RE CROSSING THE MIGHTY OHIO RIVER AND INTO LOUISVILLE, KENTUCKY!

THEY STILL MAKE LOUISVILLE SLUGGER WOODEN BASEBALL BATS HERE. AND IT'S HOME TO THE KENTUCKY DERBY, RACEHORSE COUNTRY!

THE OHIO RIVER IS HUGE!

YEAH! KENTUCKY!

WELCOME TO KENTUCKY
THE BLUEGRASS STATE

WHY DOES IT SAY THE 'BLUEGRASS STATE'? GRASS IS GREEN WHERE WE'RE FROM.

IT'S A SPECIAL KIND OF GRASS THAT GROWS HERE AND THE HORSES LOVE IT! IT'S ACTUALLY GREEN, BUT HAS BLUE FLOWERS IF IT GROWS TALL ENOUGH.

LET'S PLAY A GAME... THE FIRST TO SPOT 10 HORSES CAN RIDE NEXT TO ME IN SHOTGUN AND GIVE 'BELLE A REST.

I FOUND THE FIRST ONE! SHE'S SO TALL! AND SHE HAS A BABY! THAT'S TWO!

CHAPTER FOUR: ROUGHING IT

"*TWELVE HOURS LATER AND WE ARE CELEBRATING RIGHT AT THE PARK ENTRANCE. OUR ADVENTURE HAS BEGUN...*"

SMILE AND SAY 'SMOKIES!'

CLICK

SMOKIES!

GREAT SMOKY MOUNTAINS PARK

GOOD JOB, *PAPI*. YOU GOT US HERE SAFE AND SOUND.

AH, HEAR THE SOUND OF THE CRICKETS? ALSO, OUR OWN SET OF CRICKETS CHATTERING IN THE TENT...

WHAT COULD THOSE GIRLS POSSIBLY BE TALKING ABOUT?

CHIRP

CHIRP

THIS IS COOL. LIKE A SLUMBER PARTY FOR A WHOLE WEEK!

GOOD JOB, GIRLS. NOW, FOR THE RULES: ONE: DON'T WANDER OFF ALONE. USE THE BUDDY SYSTEM.

TWO: NO FOOD ALLOWED. A.J., THAT GOES FOR YOUR SECRET TAFFY STASH. BEARS AND RACCOONS LIKE HUMAN FOOD AND IT'S BAD FOR THEM.

AND THREE: TENT ZIPPER STAYS ZIPPED. OR WE BECOME MOSQUITO SNACKS TONIGHT, GOT IT?

AND WE WOULDN'T WANT ANY *SNAKES*, SNUGGLED ON YOUR PILLOW! RIGHT, MARINA?

THERE AREN'T ANY SNAKES HERE.

ACTUALLY, THERE IS A POISONOUS SNAKE CALLED A 'COPPERHEAD.' THEY EAT MICE AND RODENTS.

THEY ARE SHY AND DON'T BITE UNLESS YOU SCARE THEM.

GULP!

CHAPTER FIVE: SMOKY SCIENCE SQUAD

HI! I'M PRETTY MUCH A NERD MYSELF, SO NICE TO MEET YOU ALL.

DR. LISA HAS AGREED TO TAKE US ON A TOUR OF THE PARK AND SEE WHAT REAL SCIENTISTS ARE STUDYING TO PROTECT PLANTS AND ANIMALS.

REALLY? ARE YOU A BIOLOGIST?

WELL, I WENT TO COLLEGE AND MAJORED IN BIOLOGY, THEN EARNED MY MASTER'S DEGREE IN BUSINESS, AND A DOCTORATE IN FORESTRY. NOW I OVERSEE ALL THE SCIENCE AND RESEARCH IN THE PARK

THE SMOKIES ARE LIKE A *LIVING SCIENCE LAB!* WE WANT TO LEARN ALL ABOUT THE PLANTS, ANIMALS AND PEOPLE WHO HAVE LIVED HERE SO WE CAN PROTECT THE PARK FOR EVERYONE.

DO YOU SEE BEARS?

'WE SURE DO. THERE ARE ABOUT 1,500 NORTH AMERICAN BLACK BEARS HERE. WE STUDY THEM, PUT GPS COLLARS ON THEM, AND TRACK THEM ON COMPUTER MAPS.'

MOM, THIS IS SO COOL! WHAT DO WE GET TO SEE TODAY?

I HAVE A PLAN AND I NEED YOUR HELP...

CHAPTER SIX: ON TOP OF OLD SMOKY

"THE SMOKY MOUNTAINS ARE HIGH AND THE TUNNELS ARE FUN TO DRIVE THROUGH. DR. LISA WAS TAKING US TO THE HIGHEST POINT IN TENNESSEE!

"FINALLY WE MADE IT!

THIS IS CALLED *CLINGMAN'S DOME*. WE ARE MORE THAN A MILE UP FROM THE GROUND. ON A CLEAR DAY YOU CAN SEE SEVEN STATES. CAN YOU NAME THEM?

TENNESSEE! KENTUCKY! NORTH CAROLINA! SOUTH CAROLINA! VIRGINIA!

KENTUCKY! NORTH CAROLINA! SOUTH CAROLINA! VIRGINIA! TENNESSEE!

TENNESSEE! VIRGINIA! SOUTH CAROLINA! NORTH CAROLINA! KENTUCKY!

NORTH CAROLINA! SOUTH CAROLINA! KENTUCKY! TENNESSEE! VIRGINIA!

TENNESSEE! KENTUCKY! NORTH CAROLINA! SOUTH CAROLINA! VIRGINIA!

≶HUFF!≶ THAT'S ONLY *FIVE* STATES! ≶PUFF!≶

WHO SAID HIKING IS FUN?

WHAT ARE THE OTHER TWO STATES?

ALABAMA AND MISSISSIPPI!

OH, WE SHOULD HAVE THOUGHT OF THAT--WOW!

35

LOOK, A.J.! DID YOU KNOW THE SMOKIES IS THE SALAMANDER CAPITAL OF THE WORLD? THIS ONE'S A *BLACK-CHINNED SALAMANDER.*

HE'S SO RED. IS HE A FROG OR A LIZARD?

LIZARDS ARE REPTILES AND HAVE SCALY SKIN. SALAMANDERS ARE AMPHIBIANS. SO, THEY ARE MORE LIKE FROGS...

...MOST SALAMANDERS DON'T HAVE LUNGS AND THEY BREATHE THROUGH THEIR SKIN AND BLOOD VESSELS.

GREGORIO, BRING YOUR CAMERA. I NEED A PICTURE.

MY FIRST SPECIES!

CLICK

CLICK

CLICK

WELL, ACTUALLY, I HAVE AMPHIBIANS, SO IT'S *MINE.*

OH, ZARA, YOU ALWAYS WIN. I FOUND HIM FIRST WITH DR. LISA.

AS CITIZEN SCIENTISTS YOU BOTH HELP THE PARK. WE NEED TO SEE HOW SPECIES ARE DOING AND DISCOVER NEW ONES! THERE ARE ABOUT 24 LUNGLESS SALAMANDER SPECIES IN OUR PARK SO PLENTY MORE FOR COUNTING!

SOUNDS LIKE SOME OF US ARE GETTING CRANKY AND HUNGRY. IT'S A MILE HIKE BACK TO THE CAR AND THEN LET'S ALL HEAD TO THE RV FOR A LATE LUNCH OVER THE FIRE.

LET'S GO! I WANT TO CHECK MY STAR MAPS FOR THE COMET. IF WE'RE LUCKY WE ALSO MIGHT SEE MARS, JUPITER, AND SATURN!

CHAPTER SEVEN: NATURE'S FIREWORKS

"WE WERE ALL PRETTY TIRED AND THE SUN WAS SETTING FAST. MARINA WAS SETTING UP HER TELESCOPE WHILE DR. LISA WAS EXCITED TO TALK ABOUT LIGHTNING BUGS..."

GOOD JOB TODAY, CITIZEN SCIENTISTS! YOU SAW SOME IMPORTANT SPECIES TODAY. AND TONIGHT, THERE'S ANOTHER EXCITING EVENT FEW PEOPLE EVER GET TO SEE.

YOU MEAN THE COMET?

WELL, THE COMET IS EXCITING, BUT I'M TALKING ABOUT *FIREFLIES*.

CAN I COUNT THEM FOR MY SPECIES?

YES, MANY OF THEM ARE ACTUALLY POLLINATORS. THEY ARE NOT FLIES OR BUGS, BUT BEETLES.

THERE IS A SPECIAL SPECIES HERE IN THE SMOKIES THAT BLINKS AT THE SAME TIME AS MALES AND FEMALES TO FIND MATES.

IT'S A SPECTACULAR LIGHT SHOW THAT HAPPENS ONLY 2 WEEKS EVERY SUMMER.

HEY, EVERYONE! COME QUICK!

EVERYONE GETS A TURN TO SEE. HERE, GREGORIO, THIS IS WHERE YOU FOCUS THE LENS.

MADRE DE DIOS! THAT'S A BEAUTY. AND THIS COMET WON'T BE BACK FOR A VISIT FOR 600 YEARS?

ADD ANOTHER ZERO. *6,000* YEARS!

WHAT'S A COMET?

IT'S LIKE A VERY DIRTY SNOWBALL MADE OF ICE. THE TAIL YOU SEE IS THE SUN MELTING ITS ICE AS IT ZOOMS BY EARTH IN OUR SOLAR SYSTEM.

I'M GLAD YOU HAVE CLEAR SKY, NOT A LOT OF CLOUDS TONIGHT. DO YOU WANT TO BE AN ASTRONOMER?

AN ASTRONAUT ACTUALLY. I WANT TO FLY TO MARS!

HOO·COO·FAHOO!

LISTEN! THAT'S A BARRED OWL, RIGHT? *'WHO COOKS FOR YOU?'* I'M GETTING MY PHONE TO RECORD HIM.

44

CHAPTER EIGHT: THE GOOD OLD DAYS

"THE NEXT DAY WE HEADED INTO CADES COVE ON HORSEBACK. DR. LISA TOLD US THAT FOR HUNDREDS OF YEARS THE CHEROKEE NATION HUNTED BEAR, DEER, AND WILD TURKEY IN THIS VALLEY. THEN, WHEN AMERICA WAS VERY YOUNG, SETTLERS CLAIMED THIS LAND FOR FARMING."

I HEAR MUSIC!

HEY, I WANT TO TRY THAT!

LOOK! THEY ARE MAKING DOLLS!

I'LL HITCH THE HORSES. LOOK AT THE FUN AND NOT A PHONE OR COMPUTER IN SIGHT!

"DR. LISA SHOWED MARINA AND I THE INSIDES OF AN OLD CABIN...

IT WAS NOT AN EASY LIFE. EVERYONE BASICALLY LIVED IN THIS BOTTOM ROOM, EATING, SLEEPING, COOKING, SPINNING.

THE PARENTS, DAUGHTERS AND BABIES SLEPT ON THIS FLOOR AND ALL THE BOYS WOULD TAKE THE ATTIC.

NO RUNNING WATER. NO FRIDGE. NO ELECTRICITY.

NO THANK YOU!

CHAPTER NINE: TREE HUGGERS

"IT HAD BEEN A PERFECT DAY. SOFIA, GREGORIO, AND I WERE BUSY ORGANIZING ALL THE SPECIES WE SPOTTED AND THEIR LOCATIONS. SINCE HIS CAMERA RECORDED LONGITUDE AND LATITUDE. WHEN WE GOT A STRONG SIGNAL, SOFIA WOULD UPLOAD OUR DATA ON A CITIZEN SCIENTIST PHONE APP.

WOW. WE SAW SPICEBUSH AND ZEBRA SWALLOWTAILS AND MONARCHS. FOR FLOWERS, I'LL LOG CONEFLOWERS, BEE BALM, QUEEN ANNE'S LACE. LOCATION?

CADES COVE, TENNESSEE. LONGITUDE: 35 DEGREES, 35 MINUTES NORTH. LATITUDE: 83 DEGREES, 50 MINUTES WEST.

DON'T FORGET THE BLACK BEARS!

GIRLS, IT'S GETTING LATE. TOMORROW IS OUR LAST DAY AND THEN WE'LL NEED TO PACK FOR HOME. LET'S HIT THE HAY FOR ONE MORE BIG DAY!

EVERYONE GOT TO IDENTIFY COOL SPECIES BUT ME.

WHAT? BEARS AREN'T COOL?

A.J. RECORDS THE MAMMALS. I HAD TREES, AND I WANTED TO SEE THE BIGGEST ONE.

"IT WAS OUR LAST HIKE BEFORE HEADING HOME, AND DR. LISA HAD PROMISED US A SURPRISE...

BOOGERMAN TRAIL

THE STORY GOES THAT A YOUNG PIONEER WHO LIVED HERE TOLD HIS TEACHER HE WANTED TO BE A 'BOOGERMAN' WHEN HE GREW UP!

HA HA HA!

"THE BRIDGES WERE FUN, BUT EVEN COOLER, WHEN THEY WASH OUT.

TIME TO ROLL UP THOSE PANTS!

"WE PASSED PIONEER CEMETERIES AND OLD FIREPLACES. SPOOKY!

"WE HAD HIKED FOREVER. AND THEN I SAW IT.

IT'S A TULIP POPLAR AND ALMOST AS TALL AS A 10-STORY BUILDING! IT'S 500 YEARS OLD.

IT'S HUGE. I CAN'T EVEN SEE THE TOP!

IMAGINE SEEING AMERICA'S FIRST EXPLORERS, THE REVOLUTION, THE CHEROKEE, PIONEER SETTLERS... AND SOMEDAY IT WILL BE YOUR TURN TO PROTECT IT!

ME? PROTECT IT? I LIVE ALMOST 1,000 MILES FROM HERE.

YOU CAN PROTECT THE SMOKIES NO MATTER WHERE YOU LIVE. PLANTING POLLINATOR GARDENS HELPS THE MONARCHS. AND PLANTING TREES AT HOME CLEANS THE WATER AND AIR. WE MUST ALL DO OUR PART. THIS PARK, THIS TREE, CONNECTS ALL OF US.

CAN I HUG IT NOW?

"THE TREE WAS SO BIG, IT TOOK ALL OF US TO GIVE IT A GOOD HUG...

"I LOVE BEING BACK HOME, BUT I MISS THE SMOKIES SO MUCH. BUT MAYBE SOMEDAY I WILL BE A SCIENTIST LIKE DR. LISA, SAVING OUR PLANET FOREVER.

WHA--?

BUZZZ

COME OVER! ABUELO SAYS IT'S TIME!

ABUELO BOUGHT IT AND SAYS IT'S A TULIP POPLAR, THE SAME SPECIES AS THE ONE IN THE SMOKIES. IT'S SO TINY.

"IT FELT GOOD TO MAKE A PROMISE TO MOTHER EARTH. AND WE WONDERED: WHAT WOULD OUR WORLD LOOK LIKE WHEN THIS TREE GREW BIG AND STRONG, 500 YEARS FROM NOW?

"I KNEW THIS PLANT WOULD THRIVE, BECAUSE 'WHEN GIRLS STICK TOGETHER, WE CAN DO ANYTHING!'"

WATCH OUT FOR PAPERCUTZ

Welcome to the flora-and-fauna-filled fifth GEEKY F@B 5 graphic novel, "Smoky Mountain Science Squad," by Lucy & Liz Lareau, our daughter & mother writing team and Ryan Jampole, our award-winning artist, brought to you by Papercutz, the campy cut-ups dedicated to publishing great graphic novels for all ages. I'm Jim Salicrup, the Editor-in-Chief and Park Enthusiast, here to ramble about a different type of park, So, park your carcass and make yourself comfy, 'cause here we go...

The Geeky F@b 5 were lucky enough to hitch a ride with their abuelo Gregorio to one of our country's great National Parks. While I have yet to visit that particular park, I have been driven through the Smoky Mountains, and that can be quite an experience! While driving on those twisting roads high up on the mountains it can get scary when you're surrounded in mist and can barely see more than a few feet in front of you. Luckily, we were able to follow the taillights of the vehicle in front of us and came out of the mists alive.

Fortunately, Lucy Lareau also survived–see her Letter below. But speaking of parks, our special preview is about a couple of different kinds of parks.

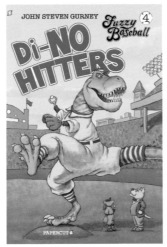

© 2021 by John Steven Gurney.

This popular Papercutz graphic novel series combines two of my favorite things from my childhood—the animals from the Bronx Zoo with the sport of baseball as played by the Bronx Bombers in Yankee Stadium. Of course, I'm talking about the Fernwood Valley Fuzzies, who are back in—FUZZY BASEBALL #4 "Di-No Hitters," by John Steven Gurney. If you thought animals playing baseball was a wacky idea, wait till you meet the team they're up against this time—the Triassic Park Titans!

So, find a nice shady spot in the park where you can sit down and enjoy the fun when John Steven Gurney transports us to the imaginary ballpark where Blossom Honey Possum, Bo Grizzly, Sandy Kofox, Jackie Rabbitson, and the rest of the Fuzzies take on the prehistoric players from Triassic Park! Oh, and you may want to take along the next GEEKY F@B 5 graphic novel, coming soon, with you too!

Thanks,

Jim

Letter from LUCY LAREAU

Howdy from the Smoky Mountains! Meet my new friend, Dr. Lisa McInnis, in the cool Smokey the Bear hat and my mates, Josie and Callagh, who help me brainstorm fun ideas for the GF5. For this book, I wanted to do a road trip and take a break from Earhart Elementary, so we headed for the Great Smoky Mountains National Park in Tennessee. Our adventure to the "Smokies" was a road trip like none other. First of all, driving through mountains is one of the most gorgeous and scary things ever. Hint: don't eat donuts before going on those curvy roads! Looking off the edge and seeing nothing but miles of mountains and trees was exhilarating. But the drive was worth it to meet Dr. Lisa McInnis. She leads scientists in the park to protect the bears, the birds, the trees, every living thing! She shared her love for nature with us, and she cares for the trees like they are her children. She is so humble with her work, but you can tell she is extremely smart. After she told us how easy

it was to get lost, I never really thought about that until we were on a trail all by ourselves and seeing how dense the forest was. After talking to Dr. Lisa, I appreciated the trip 10x more. Do you like vacations to parks? I learned that we can all enjoy and protect the Smokies, no matter where we live

Peace out,
Lucy

STAY IN TOUCH!

EMAIL:	salicrup@papercutz.com
WEB:	papercutz.com
TWITTER:	@papercutzgn
INSTAGRAM:	@papercutzgn
FACEBOOK:	PAPERCUTZGRAPHICNOVELS
FAN MAIL:	Papercutz, 160 Broadway, Suite 700, East Wing, New York, NY 10038

Go to papercutz.com and sign up for the free Papercutz e-newsletter!

Left to right: GF5 Co-author Lucy Lareau, Dr. Lisa McInnis, Josie and Callagh Sheehan.

HAMMY SOSA PRESENTS
THE HISTORY OF
BASEBALL

Baseball was invented during the **Handlebar Moustache Era**. The balls were carved out of dried moustache wax. The players all wore top hats. Batters stood on peach baskets and base runners rode on bicycles.